Is something there?
D0468298

To my son Levi, a sharp editor, a daily inspiration, and a
generous giver of hugs and smiles. This idea began with you. —L. L.

To my mom, grandparents, and favorite rocks! –A. B.

Hello?
Hellooooo?!

First published in 2019 by Page Street Kids,
an imprint of
Page Street Publishing Co.
27 Congress Street, Suite 105
Salem, MA 01970
www.pagestreetpublishing.com

Distributed by Macmillan, sales in Canada by The Canadian Manda Group

19 20 21 22 23 CCO 5 4 3 2 1

ISBN-13: 978-1-62414-6589
ISBN-10: 1-624-14658-9

CIP data for this book is available from the Library of Congress.

This book was typeset in Cambo.
The illustrations were created digitally.

Printed and bound in Shenzhen, Guangdong, China

Page Street Publishing uses only materials from suppliers who are committed to responsible and sustainable forest management.

Page Street Publishing protects our planet by donating to nonprofits like The Trustees, which focuses on local land conservation.

Can someone please turn on the lights?

THIS BOOK IS SPINELESS

(Yes. Yes, I am.)

Lindsay Leslie

illustrated by Alice Brereton

Whew! Thanks for turning on the lights!
As I said, I'm afraid of the dark.
Actually I'm afraid of most things, because
I'm spineless.

Yes, me.
The book in your hands.
I'm a real scaredy-pants. A fraidy-cat.

And I have absolutely no sense of adventure.
None. Zilch.
I don't even want to *hear* about an adventure.
Nor *see* it, nor *feel* it, nor *smell* it, nor *taste* it.

In fact, I'm on edge whenever you turn a page.

AAAAAAHHH!

HHHAAAAAAA!

What *was* that?
A moaning monster eager to munch on
my edges? Scaly, slithering snakes?
Twisting tornadoes ready to rip me apart?
See? Page turns can be scary!

You don't know what kind of story
might be lurking ahead.
Are you sure you want to keep going?
Let me state for the record that I'd rather not.

BOOOOOOoOOOOOOoooooOo!

You obviously have nerves of steel.
Well, since we're here, what kind of story do you think this is?

Seems like a ghost story to me.
Oh, nothing is worse than a ghost with clanking chains and a whining wail.

Do you (((HEAR))) something?

Hold me tight, because we need to get moving — immediately!

Perhaps this is a mystery.

Mysteries give me the creeps.

I'm a book, not a detective.

I want to stay far away from

pitch-black pathways and slinky shadows.

Although now I'm wondering whodunit.

Do you **SEE** something?

I think we're being watched from the corner.

This story isn't a space adventure, is it?
I like to keep my back cover firmly planted on Earth.

I say no thanks to
rumbling rockets and woozy weightlessness.
Yet I do enjoy the stars.

Do you **FEEL** something?
I'm a bit dizzy. Ugh.

What if this is a nature story
full of foul-smelling fur beasts?

In no way do I want to be page-to-face
with a whiffy wolverine or stinky skunk.
But a sweet bunny . . .
I could handle that.

Do you SMELL something?
My pages are starting to curl.

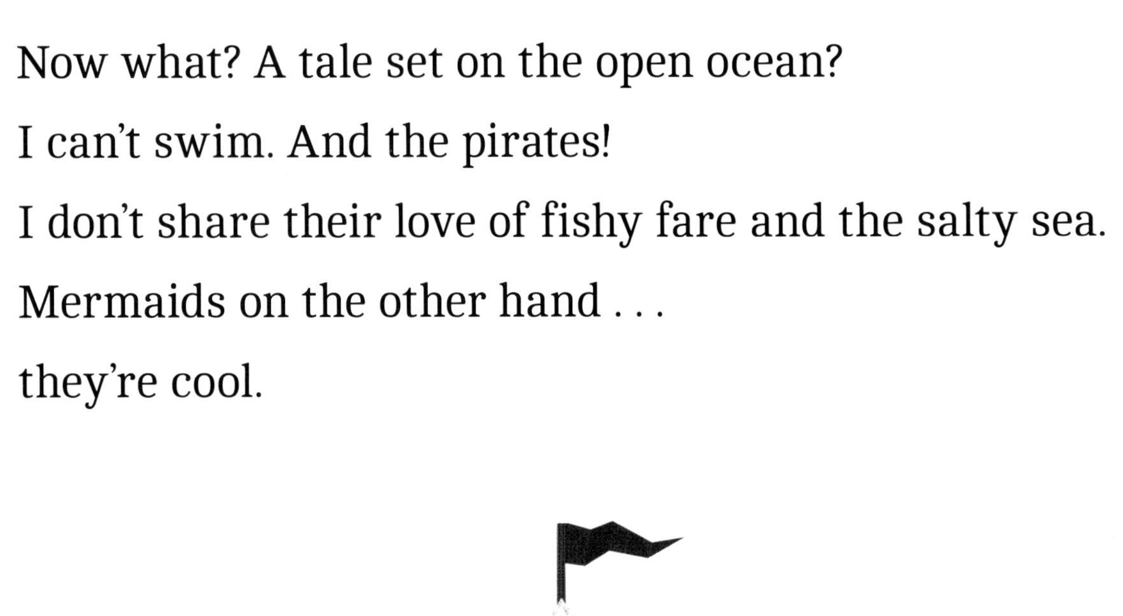

Now what? A tale set on the open ocean?

I can't swim. And the pirates!

I don't share their love of fishy fare and the salty sea.

Mermaids on the other hand . . .

they're cool.

Oh look! The coast . . . it's clear.
I think we've made it!

Oh glorious, peaceful page,
how I adore you!

And I'm OK.

Are you OK?

We're OK!

I do feel a dash more daring,
a fraction more fearless,
a hint more heroic.

I must be growing a spine!

WAAAAAHOO!

!OOHAAAAW

I guess an adventure isn't so bad,
even if you kind of forced me to go on one.

In fact, I think I had fun.
I'm only a tiny bit freaked out.
Just a smidge.

And I have a *sense* that maybe,
just maybe,
I could do that again.

Want to do that again?
You wouldn't want to leave me all alone . . .

would you?

Come back!